For Lauren and Ellie,
and all of the adventures we've shared

HODDER CHILDREN'S BOOKS

First published in Great Britain in 2018
by Hodder and Stoughton

Text and illustration copyright © Becky Cameron, 2018

The moral rights of the author have been asserted.

A CIP catalogue record for this book
is available from the British Library.

ISBN: 978 1 444 96760 9

10 9 8 7 6 5 4 3 2 1

Printed and bound in China

Hodder Children's Books
An imprint of Hachette Children's Group
Part of Hodder and Stoughton
Carmelite House
50 Victoria Embankment
London EC4Y 0DZ

An Hachette UK Company
www.hachette.co.uk

www.hachettechildrens.co.uk

Wishing for a
Dragon

Becky Cameron

Hodder
Children's
Books

Outside our window the sun has almost set
and the birds are asleep in the trees.

But Olive and Barney and Ella (that's me!),
we're wide awake and ready for adventure!

Where shall we go?
And what shall we see?

"Jungles!" says Olive.
"Treasure!" says Barney.

But I've got a secret wish . . .

. . . I really want to see a dragon.

Just at that moment, a big balloon floats up to our window.
"Hop in!" I shout and we clamber into the basket.

Where shall we go?
And what shall we see?

"Let's search the seas for pirate gold," says Barney.
And before we can blink,
the balloon swoops

up and up...

Far below is a pirate ship on an ocean brimming
with fish and sharks and big blue whales.

"Where there's pirates there's treasure," says Barney.
"Ahoy there! Can we come aboard?"

There's lots to do on board the ship,
but I still wish I could see a dragon.

We work hard, but the pirate crew aren't happy at all . . .

"We're not sharing our treasure!" they grumble.
"Uh-oh!" says Barney. "It's time we were off."

Where shall we go?
And what shall we see?

"Let's go to the jungle,"
says Olive.

And our faithful balloon
whisks us away just in time . . .

Slowly the balloon drifts down to land.
Brilliant butterflies flutter amongst the trees.

"I want to see tigers and monkeys!"
shouts Olive.

All kinds of animals and birds
rustle unseen in the leaves,
but I can't see a dragon anywhere.

Suddenly out of the shadows slides a huge tiger with two little cubs.

She licks her lips and the cubs both stare.

"Yummy," she purrs.

"Run!"
yells Barney.

The tiger pounces just as the
balloon whirls up into the air . . .

Where shall we go?
And what shall we see?

The sky fills with inky clouds.
A flash of lightning races past the balloon
and we toss and turn in the sky.

I'm scared.
And so are Olive and Barney.

"Stop!" I cry.

Thump!

The balloon crashes down in
a magical land. Staring at us in surprise
are the strangest creatures.

Ponies with candyfloss hair, pixies no bigger than teacups and all kinds of woodland animals.

"Want to play?" I ask.

We play and play
until, one by one,
the stars come out and
our new friends slip away.

"Look!" I whisper. We stare into the night
at a huge shadow in the darkening sky . . .

It's my dragon.

"What took you so long, Ella?" he says.

We've never chatted to a dragon before.
He tells us about princesses and knights,
and battles won and lost.

We tell him about our adventures,
where we have been, and what we have seen.

"I'm ever so tired," I yawn at last.
"But how will we get back?
Our balloon crashed."

My dragon smiles.
"I'll take you home."